Friends and Neighbors

Story by Kenneth Cole, Psy.D.

Photography by John Ruebartsch

 A **WE LOVE TO LEARN** Book

A publication of Creative SHARP Presentations, Inc., a project
that enhances literacy through the visual arts and art history.

This book is dedicated to all the students and teachers
who have contributed ideas for this story.
Thank you for your inspiration and creativity.

Creative SHARP Presentations, Inc.

Published by Creative SHARP Presentations, Inc.
750 North Lincoln Memorial Drive Suite 311
Milwaukee, Wisconsin 53202-4018 U.S.A.
www.creativesharp.org

ISBN 0-9770816-0-5   hardcover
ISBN 0-9770816-1-3   softcover

Printed in Canada

10 9 8 7 6 5 4 3 2 1

Acknowledgments

A heartfelt thank you goes to the Fleck Foundation as a major funder of *Friends and Neighbors*.

Special thanks to The Richard and Ethel Herzfeld Foundation for underwriting the *Threads of Diversity* tapestry shown on page 31. This art piece is a composite of illustrations of vocabulary words on community by Creative SHARP third grade program students. The tapestry is eleven feet long by seven feet high.

We acknowledge with gratitude additional funding provided by:
The Diane and Robert Jenkins Family Foundation
Wisconsin Arts Board

We are grateful to Joanne Lensink and PromoDesign for art production, design and print coordination for *Friends and Neighbors*.

Special thanks to Patricia Ellis, Ed.D., Carrie Kiiskila, Cardinal Stritch University and Diane L. Jenkins, Ed.D. for developing exercises to encourage reading involvement through learning projects at the end of this book. Thank you to Jan Lennon for editing the manuscript.

Thank you to the following:
"Hector," "Amanda" and their families
Forest Home Avenue Elementary School
Milwaukee College Preparatory School
Hmong American Peace Academy
Terry Kirtcher, tapestry artist/seamstress
Lopez Bakery
Marquette University
Milwaukee Art Museum
Milwaukee Public Library
The students who created the mosaic on page 30 which was inspired by a Simon Sparrow collage, Milwaukee Art Museum collection

A special thank you to Creative SHARP Presentations, Inc. Board of Directors

André Normil (Haitian, b.1934), The Pole Climbers, ca.1966, oil on masonite, 49" x 17" (page 8)
Milwaukee Art Museum, gift of Richard and Erna Flagg, M1991.136

Jules Bastien-Lepage (French, 1848-1884), The Wood Gatherer (Le Pére Jacques), 1881, oil on canvas, 77" x 71" (page 7)
Milwaukee Art Museum, Layton Art Collection, gift of Mrs. E. P. Allis and her daughters, in memory of Edward Phelps Allis, L102

Over the course of a year, third grade students in the Milwaukee area have offered their written ideas about good news in their community. For their diligent contributions to this book, we thank the following:

Blessed Sacrament School: *Teacher:* Ms. Mlagan
John, Emily, Destiny, Brett, Aubin, Sarah, Ashlee, Kellie, Kristine, Rachel, Carly, Sam, Maureen, Paige, Joshua, Andrew Z., Mitch, Andrew K., Joey, Kevin, Sean, Brendon and Mike

Dr. Benjamin Carson Academy of Science: *Teachers:* Ms. Strohl, Ms. Wensel, Ms. Boysen
Fayneisha , Paradise, Makya, Lashawnda, Clarence, Dajaun, Charles, Dontarrion, Reshaun, Deandre, Mohogane, Dominick, Isaiah, Traveion, Brontia, Freddy, Chezray, Alexis, Marsha, Tremell, Jada, Danielle, Diomond, Chitara, Devonte, Akasha, Laheem, Lance, Rashawn and Matthew

Emmaus Lutheran School: *Teacher:* Ms. Tischer
Monique, Donovan, Micaila, Deja, James, Cheykese, Jalaun, Demetris, Christopher, Joycelyn, Juvonnie, Dominique, Charmeek, Shanice, Janay, Kajha, Ashley, Demetria, and Whitney

Forest Home Avenue School: *Teacher:* Ms. Maas; *Students:* Josue, Dominique, Daquan, Marisela, Lydia Rea, Nathan, Selina, Amber; *Teachers:* Ms. Morales, Ms. Karan; *Students:* Isaac, Cesar, Tatiana, Jessica, *Teachers:* Ms. Smith, Ms. Danker; *Students:* Luis, Sirena, Tommie, Jamine, Jose, Harolyn, Fernando, Monica, Courtney, Jamila, Arnaldo, Jessie, Cristhian, Brian, Margareth, Michael, Amelya, Alex, Samuel, Christopher, Heidi, Erica, Victoria, Ricardo; *Teachers:* Ms. A., Ms. Morrow; *Students:* Anais, Cristian, Maria, Ramona, Veronica, Juan, Darlene, Lanish, Kiashira, James, James, Kathryn, Jessica, Yamilex, Andres, Anthony, Meranda, Maribel, Bibiano, Kayla, Marco, Andrew, Reyna, Alfredo, Jorge and Carmen

Lloyd Street Global Education School: *Teachers:* Ms. Cords, Ms. Dragotta, Ms. Lee, Ms. Schmitz, Ms. Serak, Ms. Wolter
Willie, Ceasar, Narrielle, Tove, Brianna, Runny, Mikaehla, Vondra, LeAnna, Telesha, Daniel, Hakeem, Christina, Monte, Shakel, Sammy, Bruce, Brian, Elijah, Donald, Cordell, Jazmen, Joemonnie, Felishia, Jada, Elaine, Erica, Zechariah, Ashley, Keshawn, Jasmin, Michael, Taja, Lakeisha, Xavier, Dominique, Andreaus, David, Myasia, Antonio, Mykesha, Kyree, Daijon, Charles, Steven, Jac'quel, Shannon, Keezanna, Miranda, Ayliyah, Lavassar, Dionna, Precious, Cherish, Savon, Wanya, Dalvin, Jania, Rakeeda, Joshua, Levi, Nahona, Diamond, Twannisha, Brian, Amarah, Timara, Keyonsha, Fasthisa, Darias, Shanaz, Mytesha, Kearri, Justina, Audreyanna, Imani, Elvin, Donnell, Casey and Brandee

Ralph H. Metcalfe Neighborhood School: *Teachers:* Ms. Benson, Ms. Schultz, Ms. Thomas; *Students:* Malaka, Eric, Donte, Johnnie, Shannon, Brandon, Romesha, Sharday, Meakean, Ravon, Michael, Aquania, Sherita, Shaquilla, Dayshana, Ke'ante, Earline, Eric, LaTarsha, Derrick, Ariana, Keandrae, Rasheed, Verniesha, Aramis and Chet

Messmer Preparatory Catholic School: *Teachers:* Ms. Dreger, Ms. Hayden
Bierra, Lecharanton, Trayvon, Jasmine, Maurice, Christopher, Asia, Katia, Edgar, Charmaine, Elise, Brittney, Ebony, Shantaneak, Kimberly, Marcus, Taquayla, Joelle, Deniko, Mariah, Tamia, Mykayla, Melina, Jamare', Vonnae, Cheyenne, Charles, Rebecca, Hailee, Dominique, Reginald, Don, Revinj, Landon, Kamari and Ajon

New Berlin Center Elementary School: *Teacher:* Ms. Anderson
Maddie, Alec, Sarah, Alec, Courtney, Ali, Jenna, Cindy, Grant, Kyle, David, Amber, Stephen, Jeremy, Jessa, Meredith, Adam, Joshua, Austin, Jessica, Stephanie and A.J.

Urban Day 24th Street School: *Teacher:* Ms. Suarez
Cierra, Tyisha, Deja, Nadia, Gregory, Deanna, Tony, Shunteera and Haley

Victory School for the Gifted and Talented: *Literacy Coach:* Ms. Mosby
Duwayne, Aya, Courtney, Taylor, Olivia, Samantha, Daniel, Anthony, Jesse, Giovani, Bishop, Jose, Masroor, Anna, Mohammad, Camri, Woody, James, Robert, Antioinette, Christopher, Develyn, Chrystal, Cassandra, Kristina, Issa, Deya, Renna, Vanessa, Adrian, Michelle, Dalya, Estefany, Shandi, Jennifer, Yasbeth, Trevor, Frank, Rae and Eduardo

Tapestry Project: SHARP Student Artists

Academy of Learning & Leadership
Portia and Markayla

Allen Field
Erminia and Mariéli

Blessed Sacrament School
John, Emily, Destiny, Brett, Aubin, Sarah, Ashlee, Kellie, Kristine, Rachel, Carly, Sam, Maureen, Paige, Joshua, Andrew Z., Mitch, Andrew K., Joey, Kevin, Sean, Brendon and Mike

Dr. Benjamin Carson Academy of Science
Dontarrion, Clarence, Makya, Reshaun, Sharrieff and Mahogane

Eighty-First Street School
Milo, Brittany, Rushard, Devinare, Brandon, Laurisha, Edessa and Emily

Emmaus Lutheran School
Demetris, Jalaun, Christofer, Ashley, Dominique, Donovan, Juvonnie, Joycelyn, Demetria, Shanice, Kajha, Monique, Micaila, Janay, James, Cheykese and Whitney

Forest Home Avenue School
James, Darlene, Kiashira, Ramona, Meranda, Bibiano and Manual

Greenfield Elementary School
Osvaldo, Maria, Steven, Khenia, Oscar, Luis, Valerie, Elienid, Jose, Selina, Marisol, Ana-Karen, Monica, Amairani, Maria, Daisy, Ninoshka, Miquel, Ramon, Nancy, Eric, Priscilla, Julia, Karla, Lorena, Luis, Carla, Aaron and Gorge

Lloyd Street Global Education School
Sammy, Brianna, Antonio, Charles, Monashay, Ke on, Jaquan, Franwuan, Milak and Elijah

Ralph H. Metcalfe Neighborhood School
Eric, Malaka, Quiana, D'Anna, Ariana, Torri, Rasheed, Jackson, Nuemonei, Kelijha, Dashuan, Johnnie, Victoria, Carrie, Derrick, Sherita, Drevon, Donte', Chelsea, Eric, Jerry, Dayshana, Earline, Aquania, Ke'Andrae, Shaquilla, Ke'ante, Takiea, Latarsha, Verniesha, Romesha, Rahagee, Ravon, Marcelse, Martez, Shannon, Chet, Stacey, Aramis, Meakan, Sharday, Quntella, Alexander, Michael and Brandon

Messmer Preparatory Catholic School
Edgar, Mariah, Jasmine, Asia, Shantaneak, Tamia, Vonnae, Deniko, Trayvon, Rebecca, Melina, Hailee, Charles, Revinj and Landon

Poplar Creek Elementary School
Maggie, Jonathon, Monica, Rachel, Cara, James, Brett and Autumn

Prospect Hill Elementary School
3-4 Multi-Age Classes

St. Martini Lutheran School
Lisa, Diana, Sergio, Eduardo, Erika, Abreanna, Omar, Brandy, Shelia, Destiny, Tizok, Veronica, Maribel, Maria, Andres, America, Jesus Sue, Maria and Michelle

St. Rose Catholic Urban Academy
3rd Grade Students

Urban Day 12th Street School
Joslyn, Faarez, Brianne, Keyonte, Jada, Joseph, Jaquondis, Breon, Rolaijah, Alexius, Travess, Essence, Destanee, Nathaniel, Deanna, Dedrick, Nyasia, Ra'shad, Devin, Brianna, Derrick, Shelby, Timothy, Ashley, Anthony, Kentria, Carissa, Kristopher and Krystal

Urban Day 24th Street School
3rd Grade Students

Victory School for the Gifted and Talented
3rd Grade Students

Hector and Amanda were the best of friends. Whether on the playground, in the classroom or just walking to school, they were like two peas in a pod and always together.

Although they had much in common, Hector and Amanda were also different in many ways. Hector was born in Puerto Rico and Amanda in the United States. But that didn't matter because they spoke the language of friendship very well. As the sun rose, Amanda shouted, "Buenos dias!" across the street to Hector.

And Hector replied, "Good morning!"

Walking to school, they strolled past Mr. Todd's house, "Good morning!" Next, they were greeted by Ms. Berger with a warm and gentle, "Good day."

Strolling along, Hector asked his best friend, "What do you want to be when you grow up?"

Amanda's pace slowed and she answered, "A poet. One day the whole world will read my beautiful poems. How about you?"

Hector quickly responded, "Me? I'm going to be an artist!"

Once at school, the two friends and their classmates settled in for the day. "Class," said their teacher, Ms. Phipps, "I've got a surprise for you. Today we're going on a field trip!"

The class fidgeted with excitement. Would it be the zoo? A farm? Maybe even an amusement park? Then Ms. Phipps said, "We're going to the art museum!"

"Huh, an art museum? *That's* the surprise?" All the students except Hector slouched low into their seats with disappointment.

Amanda pouted, "Art museum? Whatever." When she glanced at Hector, however, she saw that he was very excited. She thought to herself, "This is going to be the most boring field trip ever."

Smiling from ear to ear, Hector leaned over and whispered, "I can hardly wait!"

The ride to the art museum took Ms. Phipps' class through their urban community. The landscape changed from tall skyscrapers, to industrial factories, to the outskirts of suburban neighborhoods and to the many rural farms that surrounded the city.

As the bus pulled up, the children were amazed. "*That's* the museum?" they asked.

Ms. Phipps smiled and replied, "Yes, class, that's the art museum." It was the most beautiful building they had ever seen.

From the glorious architecture outside, to the artwork inside, the art museum was full of wonderful surprises. Impressionist paintings, grand sculptures and abstract pieces of art lined the hallways and filled every room. While the docent, Ms. Lennon, talked about each masterpiece, Amanda read all the brochures and educational materials she could find to keep her mind off the boring field trip. Soon, Amanda found herself separated from the rest of the class.

The docent led the class to a colorful painting and explained, "This work of art is by the Haitian artist, André Normil." The children gazed at the colorful scene of a community on a sunny day. Ms. Lennon continued, "Notice how Normil playfully conveys the beauty and diversity of his neighborhood."

Hector raised his hand and asked, "Ms. Lennon, how'd the artist show so much about his community in just one painting?"

Before the docent could answer, Ms. Phipps remarked, "That's a great question, and each of you will get a chance to answer it."

The students scratched their heads, wondering what she meant.

"Amanda, Amanda, Amanda!" Hector loudly whispered, reminding her to catch up to the rest of the class. "Come on!"

"Be right there," she muttered, scampering down the hallway. With each step and past every piece of art, she thought, "I guess this place isn't so bad after all."

Once back at school, Ms. Phipps asked, "Who can answer the question Hector asked earlier?" No one volunteered. The students' hands remained firmly planted on their desks. "Well, then, that's our homework assignment for the week," Ms. Phipps added.

Everyone listened closely as Ms. Phipps told them that their assignment was to work together and create a piece of art using materials and information gathered from their homes, neighbors and all across their community.

At first, the class had no idea about what to make, but as they listened to Ms. Phipps, they soon realized that their assignment would be quite an adventure.

Ms. Phipps explained further, "And, like Normil's painting, your community is made of so many different things that make it a beautiful place."

Two by two the students paired off. It came as no surprise when Hector and Amanda decided to work together.

The class thought of imaginative and inspired ideas like paintings, sculptures and collages. Meanwhile, Amanda sat with her head in her hands. No ideas. No excitement. And no interest. She told Hector, "I don't know what to do."

Hector smiled, looked up and confidently replied, "Don't worry. We're going to make a masterpiece!"

RING! went the bell, signaling the end of the school day.

Amanda trudged slowly toward her teacher's desk. Looking up, Ms. Phipps asked Amanda, "What's the one thing you like to do more than anything else?"

Amanda answered, "Read and write poetry."

Ms. Phipps replied, "Well, did you know that poetry is art as well?" Her teacher added, "Some artists paint with a brush, some sculpt with clay and some inspire through photography. Your gift is that you paint with words, sculpt with prose, and you inspire through rhyme. Without the words of poets such as yourself, the mosaic of the arts wouldn't be complete." Amanda smiled.

"Well, are you ready to get started?" asked Hector.

Amanda thanked Ms. Phipps, grabbed her book bag and shouted, "Let's go!"

The next morning, Amanda shouted from her front porch, "Buenos dias, Hector!"

"Good morning, Amanda!" Hector replied.

Amanda chuckled at the funny hat her best friend was wearing. "What is that?" she asked.

He confidently answered, "It's a beret, and since I'm going to be an artist, I might as well start dressing like one!"

Down the street they went, pulling an empty red wagon just waiting to be filled with materials and inspiration.

They started collecting materials for their masterpiece at the oldest oak tree in town. As Hector gathered acorns and placed them in the wagon, Amanda gazed up in wonderment at the majestic oak and said, "I bet this tree's seen a lot of change in our community over the years."

"Good morning, you two. What's going on?" greeted Mr. Todd.

"We're doing an art project about our community," Hector replied.

The kind man listened as the two friends shared their plans for the masterpiece. Mr. Todd scratched his chin. "Hmmm," he said. Then, he left and soon returned with an old wooden box full of odds and ends.

"Maybe this will help," Mr. Todd suggested. Sifting through the box, Hector and Amanda found an old milk bottle, tools, photographs and books.

"What's this stuff?" Amanda asked respectfully.

Mr. Todd knelt down next to the old oak tree and told them that the box was full of historical artifacts.

"A milk bottle?" asked Hector. "How's that important?"

They listened as Mr. Todd spoke of his ancestors who were dairy farmers. Hector laughed, "You mean like milking cows?"

Mr. Todd told them how farms once dotted the landscape for miles around. "Years ago our rural communities were largely agricultural; and, when I was your age, I'd help milk the cows."

Amanda imagined seeing lots of cows and cornfields.

At first, the materials in the wooden box made little sense. But, after learning about each piece from Mr. Todd, Hector and Amanda were given an important and vivid glimpse into their community's history.

As they left, Amanda looked at Hector and chuckled, "Hector, no matter how hard I try, I can't see you milking a cow."

They laughed and continued on their way.

Soon, they were greeted by the friendly voice of Ms. Berger, "Good day!"

"Morning!" they replied. Ms. Berger was so pleased to hear about their art project that she went into her attic and returned with an old hard hat and several books.

"What's the hat for?" asked Amanda.

"Well, when I was just a little girl, my entire family moved up here from Mississippi," Ms. Berger told them.

"How come you had to move?" Hector asked.

Ms. Berger told them how her family and others migrated north in search of the many industrial and construction jobs that employed people across the city. "And, this hat? Well, that was my father's when he worked at the factory."

"Was it scary moving to a new place?" Hector asked.

Ms. Berger smiled and said, "At first, it was. But thanks to the strength of my family and the support from new friends and neighbors, this unfamiliar place quickly became home."

Hector listened to Ms. Berger and was reminded of when his family had moved from Puerto Rico several years ago. At first, the move was scary for him, too. But, with the strength of family and support from a friend like Amanda, this once unfamiliar place was now his home.

After the kids loaded up the wagon, Ms. Berger playfully placed the hard hat on Amanda's head. Although it covered up much of her face, it couldn't come close to hiding her beautiful smile.

Photographs, acorns, a hard hat, a milk bottle and books filled the
red wagon. Hector's mind was filled with imagination, thinking of how
each piece could be used in their masterpiece. Resting along the way,
Amanda skimmed through the many books and began to paint with
words all that she was learning about her community.

Soon, their journey took them from their neighborhood and into the city. The streets were bustling with excitement. Business people, bridges, horns honking, red lights, green lights and the smell of fresh pastries filled the air. All the different faces, sights, sounds and smells made downtown a lively place to be.

Following the smells of freshly baked goods, Hector and Amanda walked into Lopez Bakery, one of the oldest businesses in town. There they watched cookies, pastries and fresh breads being baked and placed out for sale. Ms. Lopez gave the children an old flour sack and some cookies for them to eat. "Thanks," Hector mumbled as he quickly devoured the delicious treat.

Next, they rolled the wagon into Amanda's favorite building, the library. Thousands of books lined the walls and aisleways. Her eyes grew large as she imagined the great poets whose words were well within reach and how one day hers would be among them.

"Amanda, Amanda, Amanda!" Hector whispered. "You can come back later. We've got a deadline to meet."

An old library card, a dusty book of poetry and a city newspaper were placed in the wagon by the librarian, Mr. Keats. "Thanks," Amanda said.

The last stop was at City Hall. "Ma'am, can we speak with the mayor?" Amanda asked the secretary, who sternly replied, "The mayor's a very busy man and...."

Amanda politely interrupted and told the secretary about their project and even taught her a thing or two about their community.

"Well," the secretary paused, "let me see if he's available."

Soon, the mayor emerged and took Hector and Amanda on a tour of City Hall. He taught them about municipal government and the democratic process. He even talked about philanthropy. Hector pondered aloud, "Philanthropy? A word that big must be important."

"Indeed it is," the mayor chuckled. "Philanthropy is one way that people help pay for agencies, projects and exciting places like the art museum."

Before Hector and Amanda left, the mayor proclaimed, "In honor of your outstanding citizenship and deep appreciation for our community, I hereby give each of you a key to our city."

"THANKS!" they both exclaimed. This was truly a very special day.

"Whew!" Amanda said with an exhausted smile.

"This sure is a lot of stuff," Hector added.

With the deadline they were under, it was clear they had to get to work. But the sun was setting, so they would have to journey home.

"Buenos noches," said Amanda.

"Good night," replied Hector from across the way.

That night, Amanda read through the many books and newspapers they had gathered and thought about all she had learned. She picked up her pen and began to paint with words the beauty of their community.

Meanwhile, across the street, Hector sifted through the artifacts and sketched designs for their assignment. They called each other with ideas, and together they came up with the perfect concept for their masterpiece. Tomorrow was going to be a very busy day.

Bright and early the next day, they went to work. Each photograph, artifact and trinket taught them about their neighborhood's wonderful past and promising future. "Hector, how's this for a start?" Amanda asked, and she began to read her poem:

An acorn lands upon the ground,
And soon becomes a tree.
Its roots are strong and beautiful;
It grows community.

"Cool!" he replied. Just like Mr. Todd, Ms. Berger, Ms. Lopez, the mayor and all the others in their community, Hector and Amanda were working together. Their masterpiece was truly a team effort.

The next morning Amanda shouted, "Buenos dias!"

And her best friend replied, "Good morning!"

Throughout the walk to school, Hector and Amanda were met with friendly "good mornings" and heartfelt "good days" from their neighbors.

At school, everyone fidgeted with excitement as Ms. Phipps walked into the room. Paintings, sculptures, mosaics and even a large model of City Hall lined the walls. So many different projects from so many different children.

"*This* is the most beautiful museum I've ever seen," said Ms. Phipps.

OUR COMMUNITY

Reading Is Fun

As the class settled, Amanda thought about all she and Hector had discovered about their community. "So," asked Ms. Phipps, "who wants to talk about what they've learned?"

Hands sprouted into the air like trees in a forest. Glancing across the room, Amanda was reminded of the words in her poem and realized what a great future lay ahead for all in her neighborhood. With a confident smile, she stood up and began her poem:

An acorn lands upon the ground,
And soon becomes a tree.
Its roots are strong and beautiful;
It grows community.

Enrichment Activities

Dear Reader: The following enrichment activities have been included so that you can further explore the many lessons that you have learned as a result of reading *Friends and Neighbors*. You'll find that these activities are educational, enriching and, best of all, fun!

Dear Teacher: Thank you for sharing this story with your students. The activities listed on this page will further enrich the story for your class. Take a few minutes to see how they can be used in your classroom to help your students further develop their reading comprehension, creative writing and vocabulary skills.

Artifact Boxes

Meanwhile, across the street, Hector sifted through the artifacts and sketched designs for their assignment. They called each other with ideas, and together they came up with the perfect concept for their masterpiece.

With the artifacts they collected, Hector and Amanda created a masterpiece about their community. Read the story to your students and have them make a list of the artifacts that Hector and Amanda collected. Ask your students to use their imagination and illustrate with a drawing, painting, mosaic, tapestry or collage what they think the masterpiece might look like. Have your students share their masterpieces with you and the other students. Discuss with your students how a collection of artifacts like Mr. Todd's can reveal a great deal about people, history and culture.

Skill focus areas: critical thinking, listening, writing, discussing and creating a piece of art.

Dear Hector, Dear Amanda

Hector and Amanda were the best of friends. Whether on the playground, in the classroom, or just walking to school, they were like two peas in a pod and always together.

Ask students with which character they would most like to be friends: Hector or Amanda. Have them brainstorm their reasons for selecting either Hector or Amanda by listing details about the character in chart form or on a character map. Students should then write a letter to either Hector or Amanda expressing the traits they have in common and the reasons why they would make good friends. Encourage students to think about other qualities they look for in a friend and include any questions they would have for Hector or Amanda in their letters.

Ask students which character other than Hector or Amanda they would most like to learn more about and why. Ms. Berger may remind a student of his or her grandmother, while another child may be intrigued with and inspired by the mayor. After students explain the reasons for their character choice, ask, "What would you like to tell your favorite character about you?" This writing prompt helps your students realize the value of the many members in their community.

Skill focus areas: critical thinking, comparing and contrasting, and writing a friendly letter.

Community Walk

And, like Normil's painting, your community is made up of so many different things that make it a beautiful place.

Like Hector and Amanda in the story, your students can learn a great deal of history by going on a community walk. Visiting places like the grocery or corner store, library, bakery, fire station or police station will teach your students about the richness of their community. Like any good researcher, challenge your students and yourself to develop questions that begin with one of the "five w's" — who, what, where, when and why — to use as you meet with the different people who live in your community.

You and your students can also use the following guiding statements before, during and after your community walk:
1. Before going on our community walk, we thought...
2. Five things we learned during our community walk are...
3. After going on our community walk, we now want to know these five things about our community...

Follow up your community walk with a class discussion about all the things you have learned.

Skill focus areas: critical thinking, interviewing, researching, reporting, mapping, discussing, speaking and writing.

Best Friend Recognition

Although they had much in common, Hector and Amanda were also different in many ways. Hector was born in Puerto Rico and Amanda in the United States. But that didn't matter, because they spoke the language of friendship very well.

In the story, Amanda and Hector are described as the best of friends because they were always together and had much in common. We know that best friends not only have things in common and like to do things together, but also are caring and supportive. Who is your best friend? Why is this person your best friend? Have you ever talked with your best friend about why you are best friends? One way to let your best friend know that you appreciate him or her is to write a letter, poem or song about what makes him or her special. Include in your letter, poem or song things such as:

How are you and your best friend alike? How are you and your best friend different?

What qualities does this friend have that you admire?

What are things that you and your best friend like to do together?

When did you know that you had found a best friend? Why is this person your best friend?

When you have finished writing your letter, poem or song, share it with your best friend.

Skill focus areas: creative writing, critical thinking, comparing and contrasting, and speaking

Calling All Poets: What Comes Next?

Amanda began her poem and said to Hector, "How's this for a start?"

*An acorn lands upon the ground,
And soon becomes a tree;
Its roots are strong and beautiful,
It grows community.*

At the end of the story, Amanda shares the first part of her poem. If you were Amanda, what would you write next? Think about some of the artifacts that Hector and Amanda collected and the people they talked to in order to complete their project. Write the next verse of Amanda's poem using the information you have about Hector and Amanda's community.

For a bonus challenge, finish the poem with a verse about the people and places in your own community. As an extra bonus challenge, rewrite your poem as a letter or song about your community and share it with your family, friends and/or class.

Skill focus areas: creative writing, listening and speaking

Newspaper Scavenger Hunt

An old library card, a dusty book of poetry and a city newspaper were placed in the wagon by the librarian, Mr. Keats.

The newspaper is a wonderful resource for exploring community concepts with your child(ren). Using your local edition, go on a newspaper scavenger hunt to find the following items based on the story:
• An article about a local business
• Pictures of two different types of architecture
• An article or advertisement for a college or university
• An article about a local artist or a picture of a piece of artwork
• An employment listing for an interesting occupation
• An article about a government official in the news
• An article about a local community event
• An article about a person in your community whom you would like to meet

Skill focus areas: skimming and scanning, critical thinking and reading for information

Word Match

Vocabulary Builder Level I

1 ____ rural
2 ____ docent
3 ____ history
4 ____ industrial
5 ____ masterpiece
6 ____ art museum
7 ____ suburban
8 ____ school
9 ____ community
10 ____ construction
11 ____ urban
12 ____ landscape

a) a place for teaching and learning

b) a building designed to display art

c) relating to being a city

d) the people living in an area

e) something built or put together

f) a person who leads guided tours

g) a picture of natural scenery

h) relating to the country

i) used in or developed for use in industry

j) a work done with great skill

k) a smaller community close to a city or town

l) a written or oral record of important events and their causes

Vocabulary Builder Level II

1 ____ government
2 ____ collage
3 ____ democratic
4 ____ citizenship
5 ____ Haiti
6 ____ professor
7 ____ diversity
8 ____ agricultural
9 ____ architect
10 ____ sculpture

a) a teacher at the highest level at a college or university

b) a three-dimensional work of art formed from carving or molding a material such as stone, wood or plastic

c) relating to the science or work of cultivating the soil, producing crops and raising livestock.

d) a person who designs buildings

e) a work of art made by gluing pieces of different materials to a flat surface

f) relating to a government in which the power is held by the people

g) a country on an island in the West Indies

h) the agency through which a political unit exercises authority

i) having the rights and privileges of being a citizen

j) the condition of being different from one another

Vocabulary Builder Level III

1 ____ tapestry
2 ____ artifacts
3 ____ brochure
4 ____ Impressionist
5 ____ mosaic
6 ____ philanthropy
7 ____ abstract

a) using elements of color, line, or texture with little or no attempt at creating a realistic picture

b) a person who practices a style of painting that began in France in which dabs or strokes of primary colors are used to give the effect of light actually reflected from objects

c) a decoration on a surface made by setting small pieces of glass or stone of different colors into another material in order to make pictures or patterns

d) a spirit of good will toward people; also, donations of money to organizations or charities

e) a heavy cloth that has designs or pictures woven into it

g) a pamphlet containing advertising or descriptive material

h) simple objects showing human work and representing a culture or a stage in the development of a culture

---

GOOD READER TIP!

Reread the story and use the word and picture clues in the story to help you find the correct definition for each word.

Check your answers on page 36.
Mastering this exercise helps build your background knowledge and vocabulary.
Have fun and keep working hard in school!

GOOD READER TIP!

Skim and scan the story to help you find the correct definition for each word.

Glossary

abstract: using elements of color, line, or texture with little or no attempt at creating a realistic picture.

agricultural: relating to the science or work of cultivating the soil, producing crops and raising livestock.

architect: a person who designs buildings.

art museum: a building designed to display art.

artifacts: simple objects showing human work and representing a culture or a stage in the development of a culture.

brochure: a pamphlet containing advertising or descriptive material.

citizenship: having the rights and privileges of being a citizen.

collage: a work of art made by gluing pieces of different materials to a flat surface.

community: the people living in an area.

construction: something built or put together.

democratic: relating to a government in which the power is held by the people.

diversity: the condition of being different from one another.

docent: a person who leads guided tours.

government: the agency through which a political unit exercises authority.

Haiti: a country on an island in the West Indies.

history: a written or oral record of important events and their causes.

Impressionist: a person who practices a style of painting that began in France in which dabs or strokes of primary colors are used to give the effect of light actually reflected from objects.

industrial: used in or developed for use in industry.

landscape: a picture of natural scenery.

masterpiece: a work done with great skill.

mosaic: a decoration on a surface made by setting small pieces of glass or stone of different colors into another material in order to make pictures or patterns.

philanthropy: a spirit of good will toward people; also, donations of money to organizations or charities.

professor: a teacher at the highest level at a college or university.

rural: relating to the country.

school: a place for teaching and learning.

sculpture: a three-dimensional work of art formed from carving or molding a material such as stone, wood or plastic.

suburban: a smaller community close to a city or town.

tapestry: a heavy cloth that has designs or pictures woven into it.

urban: relating to being a city.

Word Match Answer Key

Builder I	Builder II	Builder III
1. h	1. h	1. f
2. f	2. e	2. h
3. l	3. f	3. g
4. i	4. i	4. b
5. j	5. g	5. c
6. b	6. a	6. d
7. k	7. j	7. a
8. a	8. c	
9. d	9. d	
10. e	10. b	
11. c		
12. g		

Bibliography

The books listed below have themes similar to those in the story about Amanda and Hector. You are encouraged to read one or more of these books to enrich your reading experience and background knowledge.

Art

Beautiful Blackbird	Ashley Bryan
Look! Zoom in on Art	Gillian Wolfe
Vincent van Gogh & Paul Gauguin: Side by Side The Yellow House	Susan Goldman Rubin
Micawber	John Lithgow

Community

No Bad News	Kenneth Cole, John Ruebartsch
A Street Called Home	Aminah Brenda Lynn Robinson
Something Beautiful	Sharon Dennis Wyeth
On Grandaddy's Farm	Thomas B. Allen
Farming Today Yesterday's Way	Cheryl Walsh Bellville
A City Album	Peter and Connie Roop
A Building on Your Street	Simon Seymour
A Year in the City	Kathy Henderson
City Fun	Margaret Hillert
A Car Trip in Photographs	Ken Robbins
Around Town	Chris K. Soenpiet